The Corpse-Eater

by

Patricia Correll

2018 Patricia Correll

All rights reserved. No portion of this book may be reproduced in any form without permission from the publisher, except as permitted by U.S. copyright law. For permissions contact: anakhouri79@gmail.com

Cover photo by itsmeneosiam/CCO/Modified from original

It had been raining for days. Sometimes a drizzle, sometimes a downpour, but most often in steady, monotonous sheets that turned the ground to sucking mud and plastered Rinko's clothes to her body. Illness and rain made her father unable to stagger more than twenty paces before he had to rest, and their lack of progress gnawed at her.

Progress? To where? She wiped her face and blinked at Father. He leaned against a tree, coughing into the crook of his arm. His soaked clothes clung to his frame, showing Rinko how gaunt he had become. The conical farmer's hat he wore shadowed his eyes, but as his cough sputtered to a halt and he lowered his arm, she saw streaks of blood in his gray beard.

"Father, come along. We'll find shelter soon." Rinko slid her hand under his elbow. "Some place dry."

He smiled wanly at her, nodding agreement even though she'd been saying the same thing for hours now, or maybe days.

"Of course, my daughter." And he surged to his feet with a hint of his old strength. But he leaned heavily on her arm, and Rinko began counting each plodding step he took.

The trees rose all around, dumping streams of rain down on their heads and flinging up coils of root to snag their feet. Rinko hated trees. She hated mountains, and forests, and her mother and her brothers. And that crawling worm of a daimyo, the white barbarians, the Son of Heaven, the gods themselves-

Father's foot skidded on a patch of mud-slick grass and he nearly fell, dragging at Rinko's shoulder. She planted her feet to keep her balance. Her knee twisted painfully but her foot struck a rock before she could topple over. She managed to haul her father to his feet. They leaned against each other, panting, unable to catch their breath in the relentless rain. Father had another coughing fit, not as bad this time.

Ten steps, Rinko thought, forcing down a rising thread of desperation. Samurai did not panic. She would put a knife through her own throat before she surrendered to despair.

"Ten steps," she muttered. Ten steps, then ten more, then ten more-

"All right, Rin?" Father wiped his mouth.

"Yes." Her answer was swallowed in the maddening patter of the rain. She halted and scraped her hair off her face. Her head swam--hunger made her feel light and dizzy. When she saw a hut between two trees she thought she was imagining it. Rinko blinked, but the hut didn't disappear. "Father-"

"I see it," he wheezed. He straightened up and took a step on his own. Rinko hurried to his side, to catch him when he stumbled. Slowly they approached the hut. Rinko saw how tiny the hut was, barely large enough for one person to lie down. At least Father could get out of the rain. The walls were rickety, the door framed by gaps in the planks, but the thatching looked dense enough. Rinko reached out to shove open the door. But it swung open before she could touch it. Rinko froze. A very old man peered at her.

He was only as tall as Rinko, with a weathered face and a wide mouth like a frog's. He wore the somber robe of a monk.

"Young woman?" He croaked.

"Brother." Rinko raised her voice above the rain. "We're travelers seeking shelter, only for an hour or two."

He squinted past her, at her father. "Why are samurai out in this corner of the empire, in a storm?"

She gritted her teeth. How had he known? She'd tried hard to hide it, much as it galled her. She'd even wrapped Father's swords in silk and strapped them in the pack across her own shoulders. "Please, Brother. If my father could come out of the rain, even for a few moments, we would both be eternally grateful to you." She was so desperate that she nearly told the monk that Father was sick, but at the last second bit her tongue. She couldn't humiliate him in front of the holy man.

The little monk glanced at her father, then shook his head. "I am sorry, young woman. But as you can see, this hovel is barely large enough for me. Being a hermit, I never needed anything more."

For an instant Rinko's eyes prickled, but any despair was quickly washed away by a wave of fury. She opened her mouth to curse this ancient man with his bent shoulders and cruel heart, but then Father was seized by a racking cough. The monk watched him a moment, then said, "There's a little village at the bottom of this long slope, not far from here. The people are poor but kind. They will take care of you."

Father spoke before she could. "Thank you, Brother. We'll take your advice."

The monk bowed slightly and closed the door in Rinko's face. A hard kick would splinter the ill-fitting door. And when she had her hands on that old man-

Father coughed again, and she was filled with shame. This was no way for a samurai to act. The slope the monk had indicated wasn't far, and didn't seem too steep, though it was hard to see through the rain. At least the forest was so dense they couldn't tumble downhill very far before hitting a tree. Rinko lifted one foot out of the muck, resisting its attempts to suck her back down. "Come, Father."

He nodded and managed to shift some of his weight from her shoulders.

The slope proved to be gentle but long, crowded with slender saplings that hid behind the falling rain until the humans were almost upon them. One bent under her sandal, then snapped upright when she stepped aside, lashing across her jaw. The sting made her gasp, but it faded to an ache in a few moments. Rinko couldn't tell if it was blood or just more rain that wetted her neck.

At the base of the hill the mud was even deeper, nearly to her knees. Rinko almost fell, but Father caught her wrist and leaned back, just managing to keep her on her feet. He raised one finger and pointed. She blinked rain from her lashes, and in the instant before more water clouded her vision she saw the village.

It was tiny, eight or ten houses huddled together, and beyond that fields hemmed in by more trees. "Not far now, Father."

He nodded, coughing. Rinko forced her aching legs to bend and lift. She half-guided, half-carried Father down the last bit of hill, slipping and stumbling. At last they slid to a halt in front of the nearest house. Her father leaned against the weathered planks. Relieved of his weight, Rinko's shoulder burned and prickled as if a thousand needles pierced the muscle. She stretched her fingers--the tips as white and puckered as a drowned corpse's--and closed them into the tightest fist she could. Her ragged nails bit into her palms. She paused and looked around, but nothing moved; even the livestock must be kept inside, safe from the pelting rain. Rinko pushed her sodden hair out of her face, glanced at Father, and knocked on the door.

For long moments nothing happened. She was seized by the conviction that the place was abandoned, that each of these little houses was empty and silent, and most importantly dry, so it was foolish to stand here dripping when they could be inside. Rinko forced her fingertips beneath the edge of the door and gave it a shove.

A tall woman blinked down at her. She was around the same age as Rinko's mother, with broad shoulders and a plain cotton robe. She took a step back, as if she feared Rinko might attack her. "What are you doing here?"

"Please." The word didn't come easily to Rinko. "My father and I were caught in this storm. May we come in and dry off?"

The woman's gaze roved over them. Rinko prayed Father wouldn't cough, and he didn't. The rain had washed most of the blood from his beard. The woman's lips twitched, but for the moment her questions remained unasked. "You can't come in here like that, you'll track mud all over. First go to the bath house and clean yourselves up." She pointed to a little structure not far from the house. "There are drying cloths, and kimonos. And you'll need this." She stepped away from the door. Rinko glimpsed a fire, cooking utensils hanging from hooks on the wall. Then the woman returned, thrusting a lantern into Rinko's hands. Her expression softened as she looked at the sodden girl. "Come back when you look decent."

"Thank you." Rinko took the lantern in one hand and Father's arm in the other. She felt the woman's gaze on her back as they moved slowly toward the bath house.

The door stuck in its frame, and Rinko had to give it a vicious kick to open it. Father entered without even hesitating at the dark interior. Rinko ducked inside herself and slammed the door closed behind her.

The endless drum of rain was muted. Rinko drew her first breath of dry air in days. Now that they were out of the downpour a great wave of weariness swept over her, and she sagged against the door. The place smelled damp, but it was shelter.

Father coughed again. She lifted the lantern, saw a bathing stool, and hurried to help him sit down. Water trickled down their legs to pool around their sandals. Rinko swung the lantern in an arc, looking at the dark tub, the shelf of soap and drying cloths and folded kimonos. She set the lantern on the floor and started to shift the heavy wooden cover of the tub, but Father stopped her. "I've no wish to be immersed, Rin. Not anymore, at least."

Rinko heartily agreed. She turned away while Father washed and dressed, pausing often to cough. She crouched by the door, shivering, tracing patterns in the water with her finger. She thought of the fire she'd seen in the house. Her stomach growled unpleasantly.

After a very long time Father was finally ready. The kimono he wore was faded but clean. Rinko folded his muddy clothes and tucked them into her pack. Father sat on the stool, facing the wall, and combed out his hair while Rinko quickly washed and dressed. After days in her wet clothes, the touch of dry cotton on her skin was as sweet as silk.

She loathed the thought of going back out into the rain. But the bath house was damp and chilly, and Father was coughing again, though he was so tired that this time it was no more than a weak gagging.

"Can you stay here a moment, Father? I'll make arrangements with the villagers while you keep dry."

"Thank you, daughter. I won't run away, I promise."

She left him the lantern and followed the path back to the house. The woman met her at the door. She must have been watching for their return. She looked Rinko over, decided she was clean enough, and ushered her inside. "Where's your grandfather?"

Rinko bristled. Father had been old when she was born, but she didn't like it when people made assumptions. "My father is waiting in the bath house while I make our arrangements."

The woman nodded. "Dutiful child."

Was that a hint of sarcasm in her tone? Rinko scowled. She opened her mouth to snap a reply when another voice said, "What's your name?"

She looked past the woman. A young man with shaggy hair knelt by the fire, a bowl in his lap. He was older than Rinko, but not by much--though his skin was darkened by the sun, his face had no trace of a beard. She realized the woman's sharp tone had been directed at him. He must be her son.

Rinko took a deep breath. She had to answer. The woman had been kind, and for Father's sake Rinko needed her to keep being kind.

"I'm Rin." She used the shortened form of her name, and didn't mention her family name. They'd come far enough that these people might not recognize it, but she couldn't take chances.

"My name is Taro." He smiled at her. Rinko didn't smile back. The cozy little room with its crackling fire and smells of food and tea threatened to fog her mind. She wanted to lie down right there on the floor and sleep for days.

Instead she turned to the woman. "Thank you for allowing us to use your bath house."

"Since we're making introductions, I'm Kyoko. That one's mother." She gestured to the young man, whose shoulders slumped. Kyoko narrowed her eyes at Rinko. "How old are you, girl?"

"Seventeen." Only a couple years from the truth.

"And your father. He's ill, isn't he?"

Silently Rinko cursed the woman's sharp gaze. Lying would be useless, Kyoko wasn't really asking. "Yes. A cough, that's all." She couldn't keep the sullenness from her voice.

"Hmmm." Kyoko grunted. She reached for a long, woven-grass cloak hanging on a hook by the door. "Come along, then."

Come where? Rinko bit back the words. She mustn't show any hesitation. "My father-"

Kyoko thrust an umbrella of wood and oiled paper into her hands. "Fetch him and follow me. Taro, bring firewood."

The umbrella wobbled, threatening to collapse under the rain's assault. Father sat where she'd left him. Rinko prayed he wouldn't have one of his coughing fits in front of Kyoko.

The gods were listening for once. He didn't cough at all on the walk from the bath house down the narrow dirt path that served as road between the houses. He even walked on his own, Rinko hovering anxiously with the lantern in one hand and the umbrella in the other. They followed the dim figure of Kyoko to the last house in the cluster, a dark and silent hulk that squatted half inside the tree line. Kyoko forced open the door and stepped aside, rain streaming off her cloak. Rinko peered into the dark interior. The house exhaled dust and emptiness. She helped Father over the threshold, holding the lantern out before her.

The wavering light showed her a bare room, cold fire pit, rough floorboards gray with dust. Kyoko filled the door, her cloak bristling like a hedgehog. But she didn't enter. "You can keep the lantern until tomorrow."

"Thank you."

Father added, "We are humbled by your kindness."

His voice was still deep and resonant despite his illness and standing so straight, he looked almost well. Kyoko seemed taken aback. She bowed, stuttered, "I'll have Taro bring some food too." and backed away. Rinko had to lean all her weight against the warped door to make it close.

Father's burst of strength had cost him. He sank to his knees before the fire pit and closed his eyes. Rinko left him the lantern and felt her way along the walls, exploring the house. There were two doors in the rear wall, each leading to a smaller room. Two bedchambers. It was as if this shabby house had been built for a fugitive girl and her father.

Someone knocked. She moved carefully back into the main room, dragging her fingers along the wall. Father was watching the door warily but made no move to answer. Rinko cracked open the door. The young man from Kyoko's house, Taro, stood just outside with a load of chopped wood. Rain plastered his black hair to his skull, making his big ears look larger.

"Firewood!" he announced.

"I can see that."

His face fell, and Rinko tried again. "Thanks. I'll take it."

The wood was tolerably dry. Taro flushed red when his hand brushed her wrist.

"Do...do you want me to build your fire?"

"I can do it." Rinko glanced at him. A curious expression, something like relief, flickered across his bland face. Was he that unnerved by a girl?

"I'll bring you something to eat in a moment."

"Thank you." Rinko dumped the wood into the fire pit with a crash. A cloud of old ash rose up to dance and swirl in the weak light. Still Taro stood there, rain running down his neck. Rinko raised her eyebrows at him. He started, turned and began to slog back down the path.

In the weeks since they'd fled their estate Rinko had become skilled at building fires. By the time Taro returned with two covered bowls the logs were alive with flame and Rinko was unrolling their sleeping mats by the fire pit, hoping they would dry a little. Father appeared to be dozing where he knelt. Rinko's legs protested her standing up again, but she ignored the twinges of pain and strode to the door.

Taro handed her two bowls. "Why are you and your father traveling in the rainy season?" His voice quavered, as if he'd had to work up the nerve to ask. Rinko ignored him. Hopefully, he added, "It's a good thing you found our village."

"We didn't find it. We found the monk, and he told us where it was." Rinko wished he'd go away. He looked like a stray dog, soaked and shivering, but afraid to come in.

"Monk?"

"On the hill. The hermit monk." She gestured impatiently in the general direction of the hut. Heat from the bowls bled into her chilled hands, and the starchy smell of rice made her mouth water.

Taro frowned. "There's no monk on the hill."

No monk? She and Father had both seen him, spoken to him. Her stomach growled. Taro was a fool. "Thank you for the food."

"You can return the bowls in the morning," he called as Rinko pushed the door closed with her foot.

*

The mats were still damp when Rinko plucked the last grain of rice from her bowl. It was plain stuff, rice and a handful of boiled vegetables. But after days of foraging roots and mushrooms Rinko thought it was the best thing she'd ever tasted. She gobbled it down like a farmer. When Father set his bowl aside and lay down, he left a few mouthfuls of food. She began to scold him but he was already asleep, still as a corpse except for the slight stirring of his mustache as he breathed. Rinko reached for his bowl, but shame stopped her hand. Deliberately she turned her back on the tempting leftovers, snuffed out the lantern, and stretched out on her own mat. The moment she closed her eyes she sank into a deep, dreamless sleep.

Rinko woke bewildered. She blinked at the bare walls, the bare floor covered in a film of dust that moved when she breathed. She was cold.

Then the mist of sleep cleared and she remembered. The abandoned house. Kyoko and her son. The monk. Sneaking away from their estate in the night like thieves. The daimyo's messenger, holding a scroll of creamy white paper. The second sheet rolled inside it, stamped with the imperial seal in red.

Quickly she sat up. But Father was already awake, sitting close to the low-burning fire, finishing the rest of the previous night's dinner. Rinko smiled at him, hiding a flash of guilt that she'd even considered eating it. "Good morning, Father. Is it morning?"

"It's difficult to tell in this rain. But it is morning. The boy knocked at the door earlier, but when I refused to wake you, said he'd return at midday. It isn't midday, so it must still be morning."

"What did he want?"

"There's a bit of field attached to this house, he said."

"They expect us to stay." Rinko dragged her fingers through her dry hair. It was impossibly tangled. She gave up combing it and simply tied it back as Father began to cough. She turned to their shoulder packs, to take stock of what remained of their possessions, and noticed the swords in their wrinkled yellow silk. "I forgot to clean them last night! Forgive me, Father." She bowed to him, then reached for the swords. She had the short, slender wakizashi half-unwrapped when Father stopped coughing.

"I cleaned them as soon as I woke up, before I finished my meal. They are still *my* swords, daughter. Meaningless as it may be now."

Immediately Rinko lay down the wakizashi. The exposed length of blade glinted in the dull light, the waves of folded, paper-thin steel. "I apologize." She bowed again. She'd carried the weapons for days and miles when Father couldn't, but that didn't change the fact that they were his. And it was deeply disrespectful to touch a warrior's swords without permission. She wouldn't forget again.

A rap sounded at the door. Rinko hurried to answer. Taro stood outside, shifting from foot to foot in the day's light rain. He smiled shyly and dug the toe of his sandal into the mud. "Hello, Rin. My mother sent me to bring you to the fields. In our village, every house has a field and a garden. I can help you re-start the garden, if you like."

"Thank you." Rinko took out Father's stained straw hat and clapped it onto her own head. Her cloak was only slightly damp. As she turned back to the door, she noticed Taro staring at the two long bundles wrapped in yellow silk. Quickly she stepped between him and the swords, smiling pleasantly. "I'm ready."

She followed him along a path that led past the houses opposite Rinko's temporary home. In the day light she saw there were twelve houses, all old but well-kept, with fresh thatching and unbroken shutters. Smoke trickled from every roof, but Rinko saw no one other than Taro. The rain pattered gently on Father's hat. It was light enough that she could finally smell something besides water: acrid smoke, green things, the faint lingering scent of soap on her own skin. They climbed a rise behind the houses. Rows of gardens lined the bottom of the hill behind the structures.

Taro reached into his pocket and brought out a white lump. He thrust it at Rinko. "Here."

A steamed bun, cool and doughy and vaguely deformed by his fist. It was filled with gritty, slightly sweet bean paste. Rinko forced herself to take slow bites, though she wanted to swallow it whole.

"I brought one for your father, too."

She took it with a nod of thanks. Taro scratched the back of his neck. "Rin, is your father sick?"

"It's a cough." She clenched her fist. The steamed bun squished between her fingers, and she shoved it into her pocket. "He needs rest, and to be out of this rain for a while. Then he'll be well again."

Taro opened his mouth, forehead wrinkling as if he wanted to protest. Rinko turned a glare on him, and he pressed his lips together. She didn't want to hear his foolish ideas anymore than she'd listened to the stupid physicians at home. They were not samurai. She straightened her shoulders. "My father will be fine."

"Yes, of course." He tripped over his words in his rush to get them out. They reached the crest of the hill, and he pointed. "There are the fields. One for each house, see?"

Below lay a neat grid of squares flooded with muddy water, separated by raised walkways of mounded dirt. People in straw hats and grass cloaks bent over the plots. Rinko adjusted her kimono and straightened her hat.

"Here's the piece of land that belongs to that house." Taro slid down the hill, Rinko slithering after. Wet grass wrapped around her ankles. It was on the far end of the grid, bordered on one side by the hated forest. Rinko hesitated on the edge of the water, but Taro plunged in, pausing only long enough to roll up his trousers. Rinko tucked the hem of her kimono in her sash, exposing her legs to the knees, and stepped gingerly in. He was taller than her, and so she misjudged the water's depth. She pitched forward and would have been drenched if Taro hadn't darted forward and caught her arms. His hands were rough but warm. Rinko planted her feet in the mud, cursing silently. Balance was the first and most important rule of swordsmanship. Taro released her, his face going red. The water was cold, prickling the fine hairs on Rinko's legs.

"Right now these are planted with yams." He kicked uneasily at the water, sending a wave rolling across the plot that wetted the hem of Rinko's kimono. "There should be some ready to harvest, you can feel for them with your toes..." He shuffled his feet, then suddenly plunged his hands into the water and came up with a long, leafy stem, from which dangled a lumpy yam. He looked so absurdly proud that Rinko had to smile. Encouraged, he began to talk more, telling her how to distinguish weeds from plants, promising her seedlings when it came time to plant rice. Rinko noticed the other villagers staring at her, though they turned away when she defiantly tried to meet their gazes. She watched Taro carefully; Rinko had never in all her fifteen years set foot in a paddy before, but if she and Father were going to survive she'd have to learn to farm, no matter how it galled her.

By the time they'd finished Rinko was nearly as wet and muddy as she'd been the night before. But a pile of dripping weeds lay on the walkway and, more importantly, six fat yams as well. Rinko felt a twinge of pride, despite the coarseness of the work. She'd never harvested her own food before.

"Thank you for helping me," she told Taro, and meant it.

He grinned, wiping sweat from his face. "I'll help with anything you need, Rin."

They climbed out of the paddy, sloshing filthy water over the path. Taro gathered the weeds while Rinko clutched the yams to her chest. As they started back toward the hill, a figure in an adjoining field raised its hand--Kyoko. None of the other villagers had greeted them. Rinko scowled. "Why is everyone in this place so rude?"

"What do you mean?" Taro affected surprise, but she saw how his eyes slid away from her face.

"Nothing," she muttered. At least now she knew Taro wasn't as stupid as he seemed, even if he was a terrible liar.

"They're not used to outsiders. That's all it is, Rin. One they become more familiar with you-"

"I said, never mind!"

He was silent, casting nervous glances at Rinko. As they came to the crest of the hill, he said, "There is one person you should meet today. Haru."

She waited for some explanation, but Taro offered none. "Who?"

"The caretaker of the house where you're living."

"Caretaker?" That explained why the thatch was still sturdy. But why have a caretaker for an abandoned house? In Edo if a person died or left there would be legal matters and paperwork. In the country, Rinko assumed an abandoned house would be left to decay until someone willing to repair it moved in. Why bother keeping it up in such a remote place? New people were obviously rare here.

What did it matter? As soon as Father was better they would leave this village.

Rinko expected Taro to guide her to one of the neat little houses, but instead he left the path and waded through an open space filled with knee-high grass, tossing the weeds into it as he walked. Rinko followed, holding the yams. All her muscles were taut. She kept a cautious eye on Taro's broad back. He didn't seem like the sort to try to rape a girl, but she already knew he was lying about something. At least her fighting master, at Father's insistence, had taught her some unarmed techniques to disable a man.

Their destination wasn't far. Abruptly they came to what looked like a small hill in the grass. But as they drew nearer Rinko saw it was the thatched roof of a tiny house, only a little bigger than the monk's hovel. Why did the caretaker live here, away from the rest of the village? Well, many people lived alone. Hermits, outcasts, the eta who handled dead bodies. If the villagers were as rude to the caretaker as they were to her, she didn't blame him for wanting to live by himself.

The house was weather-beaten and shabby. They went around the side, to a well-kept garden where a man crouched, pulling weeds. He was older than Taro but much younger than Father, a slight man with smears of darkness under his eyes. Taro waved his arm. "Master Haru!"

The man barely glanced up. "Is that the one I'm giving up my yams for?"

Rinko narrowed her eyes. "My name is-" She caught herself in time. "...Rin," she continued sullenly. "And we're not staying long."

Haru didn't seem offended. "You came with the old man."

She glared at Taro, who shrugged sheepishly. "It's a small village. Everyone knew you were here before you woke up this morning."

Rinko breathed deeply and bowed to the caretaker. "Thank you for keeping the house in such good repair. Do you often have visitors who require it?"

Haru sat up and looked at her. His lips twitched a little as if he might laugh, but he only murmured, "Just one." He returned to his gardening.

Rinko looked from Haru to Taro in puzzlement. She had the infuriating impression that she'd been dismissed.

She strode past Taro to the path. Father's bean bun was in her pocket, and their dinner was in her arms. Tonight they would sleep in a house. For the moment that was enough.

Taro escorted her to the door of the house but refused to come in, saying he had more work. Rinko sighed with relief as she pushed the door closed with her foot.

Father looked up, smiling faintly. There was blood in his beard again, she saw with dismay. But he was sitting up straight, and he looked more alert. A broom, a wooden pail and a metal pot lay on the floor by the fire pit.

Rinko gave him his bun. He held it in his lap and gestured to the objects. "I looked around the house and found those. It will make your work a little easier."

"Thank you." She hadn't seen them the night before, in the dark. Father began to cough. Rinko dropped the yams and snatched up the broom. "This dust is making your cough worse." Only a few swipes of the broom sent waves of dust into a furry pile by the door. Haru's caretaking duties didn't include the house's interior, apparently. Father's cough slowed, and he began to eat his bun. Rinko rolled up their sleeping mats to sweep underneath.

When she swept the dust away she saw strange dents in the wood planks of the floor. Three parallel marks. Rinko frowned. She rubbed her finger over the marks and jerked it back at a stab of pain. Blood welled around the splinter under her fingernail.

Scrapes in the wood. Like...claw marks.

Father coughed again, longer and harder this time. Rinko went to his side, forgetting the strange dents.

*

Six days after they arrived at the village, the rain stopped. Rinko had become so used to the constant patter that when it was finally gone she felt as if her own heartbeat had vanished.

"Did you think it rained all year?" Kyoko asked when Rinko expressed her surprise. "Honestly, girl, where did you come from?"

She nearly said, "Edo." For that was where the daimyo and his retainers lived most of the year, only retreating to their country estates in the summer when the noise and stink of the city grew unbearable. Instead she bit her lip and replied, "A place with a milder rainy season."

She rarely saw Kyoko, who Rinko had deduced was something of a leader in this tiny hamlet. Mostly it was Taro who delivered his mother's messages; Taro who brought her anything she asked about and often things she didn't know she needed; Taro who helped her turn over the soggy garden in preparation for planting. He introduced her to the other villagers: five married couples, eight elderly parents, seven small children, and one boy Taro's age who babbled and drooled like a baby. No other unmarried young men, and the only girls were still playing with dolls. No wonder he'd been so glad see Rinko. He must have been terribly lonely, she realized with a flash of sympathy.

The other villagers began to offer simple greetings, but never spoke to her beyond that. None of them ever came to the end of the row of houses, where Rinko and her father lived half-tucked inside the forest's embrace. Only Taro came to the door and talked respectfully with Father on the days he felt well enough to sit in the door, washing beans or knotting cord, anything he could do to ease Rinko's burden. Taro never asked where they were from or why they'd been slogging through the forest. All the same, Rinko felt him waiting, alert for any clue they might let slip. Like a dog waiting beneath a table for a piece of fish to fall from someone's chopsticks.

Father's cough grew better, she thought. Only occasionally did he succumb to the ugly, violent hacking that made his entire body shake and stained his mouth with blood.

One evening Rinko came in from their little garden, caked in mud to her knees and elbows. She sat in the door, cleaning off the muck with water from their single pail. Father watched her from his seat by the fire. It was roaring despite the warm weather, for lately

Father was always cold. When she'd closed the door he said, "A samurai girl coated in mud and sunburned like a peasant."

Rinko had never heard that thread of bitterness in his voice before. She swallowed hard. "We're only reduced to this because of the weakness of others."

The Emperor, the daimyo, the defeated samurai who'd rolled over like dogs showing their bellies, exchanging honor for their lives. But even more she hated the ones who'd refused, who'd fought the emperor's soldiers and died, or who'd slit their bellies rather than submit. They made Father ashamed.

Father had begged Rinko to submit with the rest of their family, Mother and Second Mother and her older brothers. But she was determined to commit seppuku with him; it was her right. And she'd seen in his eyes something utterly unfamiliar to her--fear. It was the one thing he couldn't bear. And so he sacrificed his pride to flee into the forest instead of dying with courage. And Rinko, having seen his fear, could do nothing but go with him.

Father made no reply to her now. He barely spoke the rest of the day, ate almost nothing of the meager dinner Rinko prepared, and departed to bed without a word. She lay awake most of the night, listening to him coughing. He'd stored the swords in his room, at the foot of his sleeping mat. For a shameful moment Rinko wondered if she could sneak in and take the weapons, hide them. She curled on her side, pulling the blanket over her head to stifle the sounds of Father's distress. She was wicked, unworthy--Father's life was his own to take, if he saw fit. *But surely he won't*, a treacherous voice whispered in her mind. *Knowing that after you burn him you'll put a knife through your own throat*. The grim thought was comforting enough to usher her into a fraught, broken sleep.

*

Wake, breakfast, to the field, lunch--if there was enough food, and Taro seemed uncannily able to sense when there wasn't, and brought extra--then to the garden and household chores. Some days she borrowed Taro's fishing rod and brought back a fish or two from the stream that meandered past the back of the house.

Some of the villagers began to nod to her when they passed on the trail. Maybe they thought she was going to stay.

And she was, for a little while. The end of the rainy season had not helped Father as much as Rinko had hoped. She'd thought the summer sun would lend him strength, but instead it seemed to sap it. The days when he could help her became rare. His hands shook too badly to break beans. In the mornings she found him lying on his side, the floor by his head splattered with blood. She wiped it up, but couldn't get the blood trapped in the cracks between the floorboards, where it blackened and dried. A heavy weight settled in Rinko's chest. She ignored it as best she could. There was enough menial work that she could let planting and harvesting and washing and sweeping and cooking dull her mind even as it occupied her fingers.

She learned quickly; she had to. The day after a thunderstorm she asked Taro, "How do I fix roof thatch? It's leaking in my room."

"Haru will do it--he's the caretaker. I'll tell him on my way back from the field."

"But we're living there. It's my responsibility."

"He's the caretaker. He'll do it."

Rinko frowned. "He maintains an empty house, and when it's not empty he still takes care of it. Why?"

"You're the first people to stay there in....since I can remember." Taro suddenly became very interested in his sandals.

"But who pays him?"

"It's a village tradition, that's all. He doesn't ask much."

Rinko stopped in the middle of the path. Haru was as vague to her now as on the day she'd met him. Before she could demand an explanation, Taro grinned broadly. He pushed his hair away from his face with a boyish gesture. "Rin, the market in Boma--that's a big town a few miles away--opens in two days. Mother and I always go the first day. Will you come with us?"

Her heart jumped. She brightened at the prospect of seeing something different--something beyond the handful of houses, the faces that were always averted or wary. A town was no city, but it was also no village.

But... "I can't leave Father for long." She turned away so Taro wouldn't see the disappointment in her face.

He twisted his sleeve thoughtfully in his fingers. Suddenly he grinned. "I'll tell Haru to fix the thatch that day, if you can wait. That way he'll be nearby if your father needs help."

"I can't leave Father with a stranger while I go off to enjoy myself!"

Taro's face fell. "I just thought..." He drew in a sharp breath. "There are healers there, Rin." His eyes roved past her, as if making sure no one was listening. "They sell medicines. Maybe something that could help him." His voice dropped to a whisper.

The faintest flash of hope. Rinko caught hold of it. "All right. If Father permits it."

Taro laughed. Suddenly he reached out and caught her hand in his. His fingers were warm and calloused, browned by the sun and large enough to completely enclose Rinko's small hand in his.

She froze. Her first instinct was to jerk away. But it was a long time since anyone had touched her with affection, save Father, and even that was rare. Samurai parents did not embrace their children.

Taro's gleeful expression collapsed into embarrassment. He abruptly released her. "Sorry, Rin, I-"

"Never mind." Briskly she transferred her lunch basket from the other hand to this one, which now felt unpleasantly, curiously alone. "Let's go to Haru first. I have a lot of work to do if Father and I want to eat this summer."

*

"Go, Rin. Enjoy yourself." Father's voice scraped like a tree branch on a shutter.

Rinko shook her head. That morning she'd wiped up yet another puddle of dark red blood. Father's eyes fluttered briefly open. "I'm not giving you permission. I'm ordering you to go."

That was it, then. Rinko rose, bowed, and backed toward the door. She made sure she could see his chest rising and falling before she stepped outside.

Taro and Kyoko were just emerging from their house into a knot of other villagers. Kyoko nodded to her, but Taro grinned so broadly she wondered if his lips would crack. The others stared. As they set off into the trees, Rinko glanced back, looking for Haru.

"Don't worry, he'll come." Taro assured her. "Haru is a good sort, even if he's just-"

"Just what?" Rinko reluctantly tore her gaze from the receding houses.

"...a caretaker."

They started up a long slope, and Rinko realized with a start that she recognized it--she'd flailed and stumbled down it on the night they'd arrived at the village.

The monk! The memory was sudden, the wizened old man in his ramshackle hut. She'd nearly forgotten him in her new life of work and routine. Rinko stopped at the crest of the hill and swiveled her head, searching for the decrepit shack among the trees. As the others turned to the right and set off along a narrow path, Rinko halted. Slowly she turned in a circle, squinting into the dense summer foliage.

There was no shack, no monk. But this was the place where she and Father had seen him and spoken to him. She saw no clue he'd ever been there, not even overgrown ruins. Taro had stopped to wait for her. Finally, bewildered and angry about it, she went to join him.

He'd said the town was only a few miles away, but the forest canopy hid most of the sun, and the trail twisted and turned around rocks and ponds. Very soon the walk began to seem endless. Taro talked on and on, describing the town, but Rinko had long since ceased listening.

Eventually the forest yielded to meadows and then tilled fields. Rinko almost laughed aloud when she saw the town; it was easily five or six times the size of the village, but still pathetically small in her eyes. The market they'd hiked so long to reach was only a dozen stalls. Rinko felt a sharp tug of longing for the narrow, crooked, crowded streets of home, so strong she had to pause and catch her breath. But she hid her amusement until Taro proudly pointed and declared, "There it is!" Then she couldn't quell a bitter chuckle.

"What is it, Rin?"

"This place, it's nothing compared to my home. It would take more than a day to walk from one end of my city to the other."

"Really?" Taro's eyes widened. "Where is that?"

"Edo," she replied without thinking, and too late pressed her lips tight. Luckily the other villagers had already scattered through the market and didn't hear.

Taro's mouth dropped open. "Edo? You left Edo to travel out here? Even the gods don't pay attention to us, but in Edo-"

"It doesn't matter." She forced her weary legs to move faster, past him.

But he was taller, and caught up in two strides. "Rin, did you bring any...money? Or anything to trade?"

"I have enough." She'd brought a few coins from Father's dwindling stash. And a jade comb, elaborately carved, though she doubted this place could offer anything of equal worth.

"I wasn't sure, but that morning I saw you had two s-"

Rinko tensed. Father's swords! Had he seen them? They'd been wrapped up, but their shapes were distinctive.

"-silk pieces," he finished. "Because usually there's a healer here, and she sells all sorts of medicine, maybe even for the bloody...I mean, for a cough like your father has."

Rinko stepped around a pile of dried ox dung, affecting disinterest. But her heart quickened. Maybe this country healer would know something the city physicians hadn't.

She went directly to the stall filled with bundles of dried herbs and clay pots painted with mysterious markings. The old woman kneeling behind the display was as brown and uneven as one of her pots. She offered Rinko and Taro a gap-toothed smile. "What might you need from me? You both look healthy enough. I don't sell love charms."

Rinko gritted her teeth as Taro blushed. "I need something for a cough."

"What kind of cough? A spring cough, a dry cough, a tickling cough?"

She swallowed. "The bloody cough."

The lines on the healer's face deepened. "There's no curing that one, you know. I have some things that might ease the pain a bit, but that's all anyone can do."

"Yes, please." Rinko's hands trembled as she reached for the folded cloth packets the woman handed to her. They smelled bitter and made her eyes sting.

"Make sure you give an offering at the temple," she instructed Rinko. "The god who resides there is said to cure some illnesses. Maybe you'll be lucky."

"I can show you where the temple is!" Taro said eagerly. For once Rinko was glad of his attention. It distracted her from the weight of the slim packets in her hands.

They made their offerings at the temple. Rinko clapped and bowed and prayed with all the fierce reverence she could muster. A shrine maiden offered to write her request on a wooden prayer card, but Rinko took the brush herself and wrote it in brisk, angry strokes. The girl hung it on a rack with dozens of others, which clicked gently together in the breeze.

"I didn't know you could read and write!" Taro was still staring at her as they passed beneath the red shrine gate. She ignored him. Bitterness had settled over her even as she scribbled her prayer in a hand her calligraphy instructor would have wept to see. Why had she bothered to come to the shrine? The gods were allowing the Son of Heaven to destroy his own country, what could they possibly care for Father?

Taro touched her arm awkwardly, pressing just hard enough to get her attention. "Rin...if anyone could make your father well again through will alone, it's you."

It didn't raise her spirits, but his expression was so earnest that she managed to dredge up a half-hearted smile.

In the late afternoon they started back to the village. The summer day was long, but beneath the trees all was dim and crowded with shadow. Rinko and Taro walked in silence behind the other villagers. The packets she'd tucked inside her kimono crumpled and bent with each step.

Darkness settled over the forest as they neared the village. Rinko harbored a vague pride that even in the gathering gloom she now recognized some of the streams, the rocks, the path. They finally reached the top of the slope where the monk's hovel had been--she was sure it had been there. Rinko paused, again searching for clues, but if there were any they were hidden by the coming night.

Kyoko and the others were several strides ahead. Rinko suspected they'd left her alone with Taro most of the day by design, but she was too tired and discouraged to be annoyed.

Rinko and Taro had just started down the slope when Rinko heard rustling in the undergrowth. She froze, nerves suddenly humming. Her weariness evaporated. Taro halted, frowning. "Rin? What's-"

She held up her hand for silence, as her tutors used to do, and found it worked on Taro as well as it had on her. Rinko held her breath, straining to listen. What was moving around the forest at night, so close to a group of humans? Rabbits, boar, owls, the strange old monk Taro insisted didn't exist? The noise came again, and she concentrated, trying to determine the thing's size by its sounds. Taro stared at her with wide eyes. The fear on his face made the hair on the back of her neck prickle. Did he know about something in the forest? Something he hadn't told her?

A bank of weeds next to Rinko parted, and something shot out of them, skittering onto the path directly in front of her. Rinko braced her feet and raised her hands. Taro jumped and backed away.

The creature stopped on the path and regarded them, twisting nervously from one to the other. It was a dog, Rinko saw, no larger than the pampered, fluffy beasts the noblewomen liked to keep as pets. But this wasn't one of those handsome creatures. The dog's fur was long, of an indistinct muddy color in the dimness, tangled with leaves and snapped-off twigs.

Rinko took a cautious step toward the animal. It didn't growl or snap or run. It watched quietly as she stepped around it to continue on her way. Taro began to laugh. She scowled at him. "What's funny?"

He pointed. Rinko turned and saw the dog creeping after her. It stopped when she did, head hanging but eyes turned hopefully up. Taro grinned. "It's looking for a master. Or a mistress."

"I can barely feed my father and myself." Rinko glared at the sorry mongrel for a moment, then turned on her heel and stalked away. Taro followed, glancing back often. Rinko gritted her teeth and refused to look. Did she not have enough troubles? This stupid dog was too small to be useful, too small and too cringing to do anything but eat what little food they had and be a nuisance.

"Don't feed it," Taro advised when they parted ways at the door of his house. "It will go away soon enough when it sees you won't take care of it. Still, I think you should keep it."

"You should keep it instead."

"It doesn't want to be *my* dog." Taro hesitated. The others had scattered to their homes, and Kyoko had closed the door, so they were alone. "Rin-"

She waited, suddenly tense. Taro's lips twitched. After an impossibly long moment he sighed. "I hope the medicines help your father."

"Thank you." Rinko felt a twinge of something she didn't recognize. She decided it was relief as she walked the short path to her own borrowed house. She felt rather than heard the dog padding after her.

She was surprised to see a faint flicker of light as she approached. The door stood open, and she could see a little firelight around the dark figure in the doorway.

"Father?" she gasped. She forgot the dog in a rush of mingled fear and hope. She began to run, skidding to a stop before the door. Father stood with one arm braced against the doorframe. His gray hair was loose and wild, his eyes wide. His cheeks flushed scarlet above his beard. In one hand he gripped the katana, which flashed bright with reflected firelight. The wakizashi dangled from the hand that supported him.

He stared at her glassy-eyed, unrecognizing. Hope foundered. "Father, it's me, Rinko." She approached cautiously, aware of the deadly katana in his fingers. "Father, I'm glad to see you're up." This was the longest she'd seen him standing in weeks.

"Rinko?" His eyes darted to her face. "There you are. Did you see it?"

"See what?" Reassured that he knew her, Rinko ventured closer.

"The black beast," he replied, and collapsed. The katana fell outside, into the path.

She snatched it up, glancing over her shoulder to make sure no one had seen. Every door was shut, and only the little dog watched from where it had retreated into the weeds.

Rinko had to step over her father to lay the swords inside; his limp fingers surrendered the wakzashi with no resistance. She knelt and maneuvered her shoulder under his arm, and thus managed to half-carry, half-drag him inside. She brought his mat from his room and rolled him onto it. His sunken cheeks were unnaturally red in the firelight. He coughed, and Rinko quickly tilted his head to the side so that the blood dribbled from his lips onto the mat.

"Rin," he gasped. "I heard it, stalking around the house. A black creature, large as a bear. Did you see it?"

"There's a sorry little dog outside, sneaking around looking for food. That's all." She wiped sweat from his brow. She remembered she'd left the door open, and looked up to see the dog had slipped inside and now cowered in a corner. Rinko rose, ignoring the dog, and shut the door.

He turned his head to peer at her. "No, it was no dog. I spied it out the window...it was unnatural. I caught up my weapons and ran to the door, but it was gone. Gone..."

Rinko couldn't imagine him running anywhere, not for a long time now. Whatever it had been had startled him badly. He coughed again, and Rinko knelt by his side. "I'm sorry, Father. I saw only the dog."

He didn't answer, and she thought he'd drifted off. She removed the packets of medicine and laid them in a row by the fire. The dog still quivered in its corner. She'd just opened the door to chase it back outside when Father spoke. "Is that...dog?"

"Yes, I'm just putting it out now."

"Let...it...stay. Protect you."

She wanted to laugh at the thought of this wretched cur protecting anyone, but she closed the door. Father mumbled something else. "What did you say?"

"Watching...me." He coughed weakly. "Black beast. It was...watching me."

*

The dog, when the mud was washed off, proved to be a curious mix of gray and black, with ears that wouldn't quite stand up and long-lashed brown eyes. Rinko had to push aside matted, wavy fur to discover that it was, in fact, female. She called the animal Kana, after a servant she'd once had with the same sad eyes.

"If it was a male, I would have named the cur after the emperor," she told Father.

Father lowered his eyebrows and frowned at her, but didn't scold. Despite the healer's herbs he coughed more than ever, and more often bloody. It left his throat so raw that even whispering hurt. So Rinko spent long days hearing no voices but her own and Taro's.

"I'm glad you can't speak," she told the little dog. They sat on one of the dirt walkways, eating lunch. Rinko dangled her feet in the muddy water. Kana nibbled delicately at a hunk of the fish Rinko had speared that morning in the stream. To Rinko's relief the little dog had proven that she didn't eat all that much. Rinko grudgingly rubbed her folded ears. "You yap at everything. You'd never shut up."

The dog jerked away and swung around, the tip of her tail quivering. Her high-pitched barks came in bursts like the chopping of an ax. One of the villagers passed by, nodding to Rinko and making a wide circle around Kana, who backed away. Rinko shook her head. "Cowards, all of you."

Taro came up the path, carrying an armful of weeds. "That mighty creature would scare anyone away."

"She wakes me almost every night, barking and barking at nothing." Rinko didn't tell him how she went to the window and cracked the shutters, peering into the darkness. Searching for the black beast. Nor did she reveal that Kana's incessant noise never woke Father. Every morning found him still asleep, his mouth open, gaunt cheeks flushed vivid red. His eyelids were a map of purple veins. His breathing still came though, harsh and shallow. "But Father likes her, I think. As long as he likes her, she can stay. Where is your father? You never speak of him."

"My father died when I was young." Taro shifted his load. "He was chopping wood at the edge of a ravine, slipped and fell, and hit his head."

"Why don't you have a memorial tablet for him, then? Or even an altar?" She'd been in Kyoko's house to return borrowed items and had seen neither. "Doesn't this village respect its ancestors?"

"Of course we do!" Taro sounded shocked, but his gaze was fixed on the limp weeds in his hands. "It's...a tradition here, not to have an altar. It doesn't mean we don't respect the dead."

Rinko shrugged. This place's strangeness wearied her. And she had more important worries. "I have to look in on my father."

"I'll finish your work so you don't have to come back," he called after her. Kana barked once, as if in thanks, as Rinko pulled her feet from the water and slipped them into her sandals. Kana followed at her heels as always, so close that Rinko stumbled over her more than once.

She opened the door of the house and was struck by a cloud of heat that drew sweat from her brow. The fire she'd built up that morning still crackled and flared, flooding the room with warmth. She'd opened one of the windows before leaving, but it did little to dispel the heat. Father lay where she'd left him by the fire pit, buried beneath two blankets. The bowl of boiled rice she'd prepared sat untouched by his head. She bent over him, anxiously watching his face. His skin had taken on an ashy color, except for his bright cheeks. Her throat tightened. After an eternity his eyelids fluttered, though they didn't open. Rinko breathed out.

Kana, who'd been lying panting by the door, abruptly jumped up and began to bark. Father's eyes jerked open. His face twisted and he coughed. It was a thick, ugly cough, and Rinko rushed to put a hand on his bony back and help him sit up. Blood flew from his lips in flecks. Rinko bit her lip, letting the pain dry her tears as his frail body jerked in her arms. Bright red blood flowed over his lips and into his beard as his cough finally shuddered to a halt.

The dog was still barking shrilly. During Father's fit she'd dashed to the door and now jumped and clawed at it. "Shut up!" Rinko yelled, but Kana ignored her.

Rinko stalked over and threw open the door. "Go outside then!"

Kana flung herself out the door and charged around the corner of the house, toward the forest, where Rinko could still hear her barking madly. Sudden uneasiness seized her. She glanced back at Father, but he appeared to be asleep. She followed the dog outside.

The summer sun was cooler than the interior of the house. Her neck and forehead prickled as sweat dried on her skin. Kana's yapping led her around the house, to the edge of the garden now lined with drooping eggplants. Rinko stepped carefully around them. "Kana!"

The dog stood stiff, staring at a figure that swayed in the shade of the trees. Rinko's mouth dropped open in surprise. It was the monk who'd directed them to the village months before. His wizened face hovered above a filthy brown robe, probably the same one he'd been wearing then. His mouth twitched as he looked at Kana. He raised one bare foot off the ground, aiming at her shaggy head.

"Kana! Come!" Rinko shouted. For once the dog obeyed, trotting over to sit at her feet. She quieted, but Rinko felt her trembling convulsively against her ankles. Rinko turned to the shadowed monk. "Where were you? I tried to find you again. What happened to your house? Why does Taro insist you don't exist?"

The monk stared at her, eyes blank. Rinko wanted to run over and shake him like a naughty child, she wanted to slap his wrinkled face. Why didn't he answer? She opened her mouth to yell, to insult and curse him and his unsettling, expressionless gaze.

But the old man spoke first. "Is your father well?"

His tone was flat. His face barely moved. An icy fist of dread clutched at Rinko's heart, replacing anger with fear.

Rinko hated being afraid. Keeping an eye on the monk, she bent and scooped Kana into her arms. The dog quivered, whiskers twitching.

"Go away," Rinko snarled at him.

The monk smiled. His lips parted, revealing broken yellow teeth. There was nothing friendly about the smile.

"I said go away!" Rinko raised her voice. She took a threatening step toward the old man. Kana strained against her arms, growling low.

His eyes seemed to sink further into his face. Still smiling, he turned and shuffled into the trees. In only a moment the darkness beneath the branches swallowed his stooped figure. Even after he was out of sight Rinko continued to glare, holding Kana in front of her as if the dog was a weapon. Kana made no move to jump down from her arms. Just as Rinko allowed herself to relax and turn away, there came a crashing sound, as if something large was forcing its way through the undergrowth. Rinko froze, looking back over her shoulder. But the noise subsided almost immediately. Was the wretched little man trying to frighten her? She snorted in derision. Kana finally stopped whining, and Rinko set her down. The dog skittered back to the house and Rinko followed. Later she'd confront Taro; she'd seen the monk twice now. He couldn't deny the man existed anymore. Later she would force some truth from him.

*

But it turned out there was no time for truth. That very night Rinko woke to coughing that was somehow both explosive and strangled. She rushed to Father's room. Her yellow lantern showed bright red blood soaking not only his beard but also his blanket, a stain that spread as more blood flew from his lips with every spasm. After a time he finally collapsed, eyes closed. He didn't stir when Rinko called him, and his breath came in soft, stuttering gasps. She turned his head to the side, in case the torrent of blood came again, and wiped his face. She replaced his blanket with her own clean one. Then, with nothing more to do, Rinko crouched in the corner, watching him, her hands trembling.

As the summer sun rose, Rinko knelt in the dust before the house's open door. She paused in her work, straining to hear Father's breaths, which didn't come as often as she would have liked. Between her knees she clutched a wooden pail. The water inside was cloudy red. Beneath the surface her hands kneaded Father's blanket. Overnight the blood had dried, making the cloth stiff and brown. Rinko stared fixedly at the bucket, at the clouds of red mist that bloomed with every push. She stopped again to listen.

Something touched her arm and she jerked away, splashing water across the doorstep and nearly overturning the bucket. Taro crouched beside her, the space between his eyes crinkled in concern. "Rin? Are you all right? I've been talking to you for a while but you acted like you didn't hear me."

She hadn't. She stared at him and wiped her hands on her kimono. Out of the water, her fingers began to stiffen and ache.

"Why are you crying?" Taro glanced nervously at the open door.

Surprised, Rinko rubbed her cheek with her wrist. The skin was slick. She'd been so focused on her task and on listening for Father that she hadn't noticed. She took a deep breath, scrubbed her face with her sleeve, and sat up straighter, schooling her features into a serene mask, the way she'd been taught so long ago.

Taro reached for the bucket. He plunged his hand inside and lifted the sodden blanket out of the water, offering her a sad smile. "I'll hang this up to dry for you."

Rinko looked at him. She looked at the brown stain on the blanket. Inside, Father's breath whined faintly. Her throat closed up and she burst into tears.

"Rin!" Taro looked around for somewhere to lay the blanket, finally settling on dropping it back into the bucket with a splash. Dimly she saw him kneel in front of her, and then felt warm pressure as he folded her hands in his.

It felt shamefully good to cry, like taking a tea kettle off the fire. She'd never realized how many tears had built up over the past months. Now she sobbed brokenly, for Father, for her lost mothers and brothers, for the destruction of her world and their abandonment by the gods. Taro said nothing, only held her hands while she wept.

After a long time she ran out of tears. Rinko sagged, feeling as hollowed-out as a melon rind. The skin of her face was stiff with dried salt, and the collar of her kimono was damp. Suddenly she remembered Father. She sat up, pulling away from Taro, who released her reluctantly. Rinko tilted her head, listening. Finally her father's breath limped through the door, ending with a gruff rasp.

Taro sat back on his heels. He tugged at the sleeves of his kimono. "I guess...you're really worried about him, huh?"

"You can't understand."

"My father died too, you know." Taro sounded hurt. "I mean, I don't mean your father is-"

"No. He is." Something had settled inside her. For the first time Rinko let the thought live in her mind, not strangling it immediately. It still turned her stomach, but she found the prospect easier to bear now. That Taro had witnessed her crying fit embarrassed her, so she kept her tone brisk as she added, "Where is this village's cemetery?" Silently she hoped it wasn't in the forest.

Taro lurched to his feet, nearly upsetting the bucket again. He caught it by the handle. "Sorry." When Rinko continued to stare at him, he muttered, "We don't have one here."

No cemetery? Where did they bury their dead? Even ashes had to be interred somewhere. No altars, no memorial tablets, no cemetery. What was wrong with these people? An idea made her gasp in horror. "You leave them in the forest? For the animals?"

"What? No! It's complicated, Rin. I'll talk to my mother, she can explain it better than I can." Taro dug the toe of his sandal into the dirt.

Inside, Father groaned. Rinko got to her feet, pausing with one hand on the door. "You tell Kyoko then, to come and explain. Tell her she can explain everything about this place, because you've been keeping things from me."

Taro winced. "Rin-"

"I have to go." She reached for the door, so angry she could barely look at him. So she didn't see when he reached for her. She jumped when his big hands grasped her shoulders. She was so surprised that for an instant all her training fled her mind, and she had no time to strike him before he spun her around and kissed her.

Rinko froze in shock. She'd had a betrothed, of course, since she was a year old. But she'd only met him twice and couldn't remember his face. No one had ever dared kiss her before. She clenched her fist and drew back her arm to punch Taro. Yet she hesitated.

His lips were warm and it was...comforting...somehow, to feel the weight of his hands on her shoulders. He must have sensed her uncertainty, for he drew away. Staring at his dusty feet, he mumbled, "Rin-"

Rinko went inside and slammed the door shut. Her heart pounded so fast she felt light-headed. Father rasped and moaned softy. She went to him. Kana, who'd been lying on her side in a patch of sunlight, rose and padded over to them. She sat and leaned against Rinko's leg.

She watched Father's chest rise and fall in short, sputtering breaths. The room smelled like metal, like blood. She touched his hand where it lay on the blanket. It was limp and cold, his skin as thin as paper. "I wish you knew I was here, Father. I need your advice."

No answer but the low scraping from his chest. Kana lifted one paw and pressed it tentatively into Rinko's knee. She reached down and pulled the scruffy little dog onto her lap, pressing her cheek into the rough fur of Kana's head. The dog's heart beat against her own chest, and Rinko lulled herself by counting the beats, twice as fast as her own.

*

Kyoko didn't come that night. Nor did anyone else. Rinko fell into a fractured sleep, hating every one of them yet savagely gratified by this proof of their cowardice.

The next day she didn't leave the house. She didn't want to see Taro. And by afternoon Father had gotten worse. His coughing fits became longer and more frequent. He'd barely moved the past two days, but now he twisted and writhed as he coughed, his entire body arching. Blood flew from his lips in vivid red drops.

"Father!" Rinko knelt beside him, frozen in indecision. "Father?"

He didn't respond. His eyes were half-closed, the visible slits glassy. His gaunt face contorted like the mask of a demon in a noh play. He looked like a stranger, a monster, nothing like the father she remembered. She realized then that it had been a very long time since he resembled the father in her memory.

Blood erupted from his mouth. Rinko turned him on his side so it ran from his lips onto the floor, where it settled into the cracks between the boards. Finally his cough shuddered to a halt. He lay still, breathing laboriously. With shaking hands she wiped his face and scraped his hair back from his forehead. She replaced his bloody blanket with the one she'd washed the day before, which was still stained but clean. She built up the fire as sweat meandered down her neck into her collar. She mopped the blood from the floor with a cloth that she tossed in a heap by the door. She fed Kana and ate a mouthful of rice that turned into a hard lump in her stomach. Then she pulled Kana into her lap and wept.

Rinko couldn't have slept even if she'd tried. Several times that night Father exploded into violent coughing that made his gaunt body thrash like a sapling in a storm. Over and over she went to him, lifted him upright, and wiped his face and beard and chest and the floor. She used every cloth she could find, even the spare kimono she'd brought when they fled their estate.

Then she waited, fearfully, for his breathing to resume. Each time it sounded thicker and more labored, as if he'd inhaled mud.

The fire burned to embers and the room stank so of blood that Rinko could taste it when she yawned. She stumbled to the door and slipped outside, Kana padding after.

A half-moon shone bright among a scattering of stars, riming the village with silvery light. The dirt path was rocky and pressed into her bare feet. She breathed deeply, smelling only dirt and green things and the faint tang of extinguished cooking fires. Kana squatted by the wall of the house, her dark fur almost lost to the night. Rinko sighed. She plucked the tie from her hair and shook it out. Her arms were leaden, her fingers clumsy.

The little dog finished and trotted to her side. Wearily Rinko scratched her ears. "We should go inside."

Kana tensed. A low growl shivered through her body. Rinko turned to follow her gaze. The dog was fixated on the corner of the house, where the forest embraced it. The fine hair on Rinko's arms stood up as she squinted into the thick darkness beneath the branches.

The dog barked, her entire body jerking with each yelp. Rinko straightened up, her weariness gone. "Who's there?"

Her voice was like a whip crack in the quiet night. A colony of night birds twittered in alarm. Something moved in the forest. Rinko swept up a rock from the path and flung it into the darkness. It crashed into the foliage, but her second rock found its mark. Between

Kana's yapping she heard a thump and a low moan. A piece of the darkness broke away and moved. Kana's barking faded to a growl as the thing receded into the trees.

Rinko stared after it, panting as if she'd just finished a sword lesson. It was dark and she was angry. Surely that was what made the creature seem so large. She'd seen a tiger once, transported from the mainland in a bamboo cage. In her tired eyes the black beast didn't seem much smaller.

Kana came to lean against Rinko's leg. Rinko hugged herself. Despite the summer warmth her skin had erupted in goosebumps. She could ask Taro what it might be, if she decided to speak to him again...

Then Father began to cough. She dropped her thoughts, scooped up Kana and ran for the sliver of open door.

*

A little after dawn his eyes fluttered open. They were glassy, but as Rinko bent over him they snapped into focus.

"Rin?" he rasped. One frail hand reached up to claw at his throat.

He never spoke again. Sometime later Father twisted onto his side. His broken nails scrabbled at the mat, the floor. His throat jerked convulsively, retching and gagging. Rinko shoved Kana off her lap and stumbled across the room, groping for some dry cloth to staunch the expected wave of blood-

But it didn't come. A trickle wet his cracked lips. As Rinko fell heavily to her knees beside him, his eyelids twitched. She reached for him, but before she could touch him he made a choking sound, thrashed briefly, and slumped to the mat, eyes half-open. After that he was still.

Rinko knelt frozen, hands raised, fingers curved into claws. Father's half-closed eyes seemed to sink deeper into their sockets. The red spots on his cheeks were already fading. Within a few minutes a gray pallor had settled over his skin.

She didn't whisper his name. She didn't shake him, cry out, stroke his hair, take his hand. Nothing she did or didn't do would matter. Father was dead.

A scream rose up in her throat, but Rinko choked it back. She clenched her fists and dug her ragged nails into her palms. She focused on the pain. It seemed to clear her mind. She stood up and bowed deeply to Father. It was hard to tear her gaze from him, but she finally managed it. Rinko turned and crossed the room to the door. Kana, who'd been lying in the corner, came after her, small head hung low, tail drooping.

Outside, the sky was a hard, bright blue dotted with soft clouds. Rinko blinked, her eyes stinging after so many hours shut up with a dying man. She looked around, but the path was deserted save for her and Kana. The air was dry and hot; a faint breeze moved the branches near the corner of the house. Rinko jumped at their rustling, her heart pounding. She stared around, not sure what to look for--the previous night now seemed very far away. But Kana wasn't barking. Rinko relaxed. She turned her feet in the opposite direction and began to make her way to Haru's house.

Kana bobbed along beside her, only the tips of her ears visible above the long grass. Rinko regretted that she hadn't ordered the dog to stay with Father. *To protect him? From what?* She was so tired, weary to her bones.

Haru opened the door of his house as Rinko approached, as if he'd been watching for her. He glanced over her body, her hair tangled and half-pulled out of its braid, her kimono spattered with blood. Her foot scraped against a stone, and Rinko realized that she'd forgotten to put on her sandals.

"The old man?" His tone was gentle.

She nodded, blinking rapidly. "I need your help. That's why you live alone out here, isn't it? Because you're eta."

"Just a moment." He ducked into his house, emerging with a box and a pair of worn sandals, which he offered to her. "You can wear these, if it doesn't disgust you too much."

Rinko stared at them. They were too big, but looked as if they would serve for the walk back to the house. She nearly reached for them. But then her hazy mind snapped into focus. There were things a samurai could not do no matter the circumstances. Slowly she shook her head. "No."

Haru shrugged, tossed the sandals back inside, and strode past her to the path. Rinko trudged after him, every stone digging uncomfortably into the soles of her feet.

Someone was coming up the path as they reached the village; Rinko caught a glimpse of movement from the corner of her eye, and a flash of plain brown work clothes. Haru ignored them, whoever it was. Rinko stared straight ahead. Kana barked once at the person, then hurried to catch up with her mistress.

At the house Haru opened the door without hesitation. After being in the open air, the metallic stench of blood was like a slap across the face. Rinko's throat tightened. But Haru merely said, "It will take some time to prepare the body."

Rinko stared at the heap on the floor. Was this Father? This skeletal, sunken thing? It looked like a puppet of a dying man with its strings cut.

"I have to get something." She stepped inside. The fire had burned down to embers. Haru was watching, so she walked quickly to Father's room, pausing briefly to bow to the husk on the floor. His swords lay where they'd been for months, where the foot of his mat had been before she moved it. She gathered them into her arms, the yellow silk sliding over her fingers. She tucked them into her obi, adjusting her balance to walk with them.

When she returned, Haru was stripping the blankets from Father's body. Rinko looked away as he piled the still-damp blankets by the door. "Take these out, girl."

She was so glad of something to do that she overlooked the order. As she carried the blankets to the door her bare toe caught on something in the floor; she looked down and saw the three jagged grooves that had given her a splinter before. She yanked her foot away and went outside, remembering to put on her sandals this time.

The outside air, hot and dusty as it was, was even more of a relief than before. Rinko leaned against the wall of her borrowed house...she wouldn't stay here, not here, the only women who lived alone had outlived all their family...but she wasn't alone. Kana thrust herself between Rinko's feet and wiggled until her wiry head peered out from under the hem of her kimono.

"Rin?" She looked up. Her hearing felt muffled. She expected Taro--it was always Taro--but this time it was Kyoko who stood before her. Her face was open and sympathetic.

The villager from the path. Everyone knew by now.

"Let me take those. We'll burn them." Kyoko reached for the bloody blankets.

"I don't have any others."

"I'll give you another." She tugged at the damp mess. Rinko had to concentrate to release her grip; she'd been clutching the blankets so tightly her arms ached. Kyoko tucked them under one arm and took Rinko's elbow with the other. "Come along, Rin."

Rinko blinked at her, bewildered. She heard Kyoko's words, but she couldn't quite understand them. The woman sighed. "Come to the bath house, girl. I've lost both my father and my mother and a husband too. What you need now is a bath and some clean clothes, food and sleep."

She tilted her head, listening, but there was no sound from inside the house. Her head cleared a little; Kyoko was offering her something to *do*. She couldn't speak. Her chest ached. Rinko nodded slowly. She handed the bundle of blankets over to Kyoko. They were only squares of cloth, soaked with blood.

The inside of the bath house was cool and dim. Rinko welcomed the gloom now--the sunlight had made her eyes feel dry and swollen. A headache pulsed in her temples. She placed the swords safely on a high shelf and stripped off her clothes. Her kimono was stiff with blood and her under-robe was stuck to her skin with dried sweat and dirt. She peeled it away like a bandage.

Her arms felt shaky. She had to push with all her strength to shift the heavy tub cover. The lukewarm water eased the stiffness of her shoulders. Rinko ducked her head under the surface. Should she inform Mother and Second Mother? Her brothers? How? She didn't know where they were, or what had become of the rest of the household.

The tears struck then, a wave of grief that wrenched out her insides. She cried in hoarse, jagged sobs, tears streaming down her face to join the water in the tub. She cried a long time. As her sobs began to stutter and finally ease, someone rapped timidly at the door. She sat very still, holding her breath, hoping whoever it was would go away.

"Uh, Rin?" It was Taro, of course, his voice high with concern. Kyoko would have told him where she was.

Rinko sighed. She splashed water over her face and crawled out of the tub. She dried and dressed and plaited her damp hair, fingers moving automatically. Last she took Father's swords, secured them firmly to her hip, and went to the door. A sudden wave of weariness crashed over her--she couldn't remember the last time she'd slept. But she schooled her expression into indifference.

Taro was pacing the length of the bath house with short, nervous strides. When Rinko emerged he stopped. His face cracked into a relieved smile. "Why didn't you answer, Rin? I was worried! Mother told me...we have to-"

"Haru is already taking care of Father. Nobody here tells me anything, but I'm not stupid. I figured out he's an eta."

His face reddened. "Of course you're not-"

"And now you have to show me your village cemetery."

"Come inside, Rin. You should rest."

Rinko bristled. "No. Show me your cemetery. I want to see where my father will lie."

"Please." His voice quivered with desperation. "Come inside, I'll explain everything."

"What's so shameful you can't tell me in the street? What's wrong with this place? Why do you disrespect your dead?"

Taro's gaze locked on something over her shoulder. Rinko spun around. Three villagers, a man and two elderly parents, stood in the path, blocking the way back to Rinko's house. Their expressions were uneasy, but she could see resentment lurking in their eyes. Resentment was a familiar feeling for a samurai to encounter. Her fingers strayed to the hilt of the katana, a gesture as automatic as blinking. Their gazes moved to her hand, and she dropped her arm to her side, clenching her fist.

"All right," she said quietly. She strode past Taro, yanking open the door. The trio on the path gaped after them.

Kyoko stood by the fire, heating something in a pot. Rinko smelled eggs and rice. Her stomach gurgled. She'd barely eaten anything over the past few days. Kana shuffled toward the fire. Kyoko set a bowl in front of her, and the dog plunged her face into it. Rinko realized guiltily that she hadn't fed Kana since at least the day before.

Kyoko held out another bowl. "Eat something. It wears on you, death."

Rinko didn't want to eat, but her stomach yawned emptily. She took it but didn't kneel. The egg was chewy and the rice dry, but she ate it as quickly as she could. Taro and Kyoko watched her, Taro's expression worried, his mother's sympathetic. Rinko ignored their staring, emptied the bowl and handed it back. Before Kyoko could refill it, Rinko turned to Taro. "Now. Tell me what I want to know. Do you cremate your dead or bury them? Where is your cemetery? I have to begin Father's vigil at sundown."

"The tradition is-" Kyoko began, but Taro cut her off.

"I'll tell her, Mother." He closed his eyes, as if arranging the story in his head. "The tradition in our village is that the body is laid out the day the person died. You were right--Haru is an eta, someone who prepares the dead. He lays them out, and the villagers pay their respects."

Rinko relaxed a little despite herself. This was similar to her own family's way. "In my family, the nearest relative sits with the body overnight. I will do that for my father."

Kyoko froze in the act of picking up Kana's empty bowl. Taro raised his head. His eyes were wide. "No! You can't!"

He was almost shouting. Rinko narrowed her eyes. He took a shuddering breath and managed a smile. "That's not exactly our way. Haru is also the caretaker of that house because it's where we lay out the bodies. All the bodies."

Rinko stared at him. "You sent us to live in a house of the dead?"

She spoke softly, but Taro flinched at the restrained fury in her tone. "Well, it wasn't always the-"

"There were no other empty houses. Your father was obviously sick." Kyoko's voice sliced across Taro's stammering.

Rinko didn't bother to answer. She saw the sense in Kyoko's reasoning, much as she hated it. So she focused on Taro, who shifted his weight and looked away. "You lay out the dead, someone sits with them, and in the morning-"

"No one sits with them. We...our tradition is that the other villagers, they, um, they leave the village for the night."

For a moment Rinko was too stunned to be angry. "Leave? And go where?"

"In the forest, there's a cave. It's big enough for all of us. You haven't seen it yet."

"You leave them alone?" Her anger had returned, stronger than before. "You abandon them? And do you throw their bodies into the forest to rot?"

"No!" Taro looked truly shocked. "In the morning, we return to the village. The bodies are...gone."

Rinko laughed, a harsh, mirthless bark that made Kana jump. Taro shot his mother a nervous glance. RInko fell silent as she realized that Taro hadn't been making an ugly joke.

"They're gone," he repeated. "The bodies disappear. Even my father, when he died. We don't know what happens to them. It's always been this way."

"Since I was a child," Kyoko added. "I don't remember any other way."

"Where do they go?" Rinko gritted her teeth in frustration.

"We don't know, girl. We told you." But Kyoko's looked away as she spoke. She was lying.

Rinko took a deep breath. She set the bowl on the floor--she'd been clenching it so tightly the rim was impressed into her skin. "Thank you for the food. I'm going to see if Haru's finished."

"No, Rin. You should sleep. You're exhausted." Taro reached for her hand, but she stepped smoothly backward to avoid him.

"I'm going to take care of my father." She turned and left, ignoring Taro when he called after her.

The death house was still. It looked just as it had before, as it had every day she and Father lived their exiled lives here. Was Father even in there? For a moment hope seized her brittle heart. She would slide open the door and find him sitting up by the fire, smiling at her.

The image was so inviting that she reached for the latch. Then she remembered, and a wave of sickness washed over her. As Rinko hesitated, the door slid open and Haru looked out at her.

"I thought you might be out here." He opened the door wider. "Come in."

Rinko didn't want to obey. She wanted to turn and run into the hateful forest, as far as she could go from this place that had taken her father from her.

But samurai did not run.

She strode past Haru. Kana stayed outside, craning her neck to watch her mistress. The eta stepped aside to allow her in. Rinko was left alone with Father.

Haru had doused the fire so the room was no longer oppressively hot. But with the shutters closed and the fire dead it was dim. In the summer heat the air already smelled very faintly of decay, sickly sweet despite the herbs Haru had placed at the head and feet of the body. She approached Father slowly, letting her eyes grow used to the gloom.

Haru had dressed him in his spare kimono, the sober black one. The white collar of his under-robe stood out starkly. His beard had been cleaned, combed and trimmed, and his hair put into a bun--not the customary topknot of a samurai, but it couldn't be helped. She would ask his spirit for forgiveness when she had time to pray.

There would be time tonight. Frightened peasants or no, she would not leave her father alone to disappear.

Father's face was gray and waxen. His fierce eyes were closed now, but Rinko saw some of his old ferocity in the set of his jaw. Haru had put on his tabi and sandals, and set his hands by his sides. Father's swords--her swords--shifted as she knelt beside him and bowed low. She should have prayed now, but her head ached and felt swollen, as if someone had stuffed it with sticky rice.

She scrubbed her tired eyes with her sleeve. As she turned to the door, the toe of her sandal caught on something. The gouge marks she'd noticed before. Something nipped at her mind, like the marks were a piece of a riddle. But she couldn't work it out. Rinko left Father and went outside.

The eta crouched by the door, stroking Kana. Rinko could have run him through for daring to touch her dog. Instead she said, "Your work is well done."

"I take pride in what I do, though it disgusts everyone else." He rose, a small man with a face like leather. "Especially someone like you."

She frowned, uncertain of his meaning. He bowed. "I'm not an ignorant country man. I lived in Kyoto once. I know samurai when I see them, my lady. Even before you carried the swords. You walk like a samurai."

"Samurai are nothing now. The Meiji Emperor-"

"We heard that news, even here." Haru said gently. "You're a good daughter, to follow your father into exile."

"What happens to the bodies?" Surely he would know. Haru raised his eyebrows, and she added, "They say the bodies disappear and they don't know why. But they're lying. At least, Kyoko is."

"It happened long ago, before I came here. But I puzzled things out. Remember, I clean the house after the vigils."

"Is it...is it an animal? I saw claw marks in the floor."

He snorted. "Animal. Maybe, but not a *natural* animal. That was a real house once, but the owner died or left, I don't know which. When the creature came they began using it for their dead. It's been a long time since there was a death in this village. So when you and your father came..."

Rinko frowned, not understanding. Then she remembered the night they'd come, Kyoko asking, *"Your father is sick, isn't he?"*

She'd known. Kyoko knew he was dying.

No one had died here in a long time, Haru said. The creature ate corpses. They must have been afraid it would move on to the living. That was why they'd taken in a man with the bloody cough.

They were feeding it.

Something in her expression must have alarmed Haru, for the eta took a step back.

"Why?" she hissed when she had her breath back. "You seem a decent man for what you are. Why do you serve such disgusting cowards?"

A wry smile twisted his mouth. "They pay me well enough and I get more respect here than I ever did in Kyoto. Besides, I'm only an eta."

Rinko saw his point. She touched the katana at her side and looked past Haru. Further down the path, by Kyoko's house, a knot of villagers was forming. Rinko knew the faces, but now instead of indifferent or tentatively welcoming, their expressions were tight with fear. Rinko glared at them. "Is there a monk who lives in the forest around here?"

He shook his head, his brow furrowed in puzzlement. Rinko turned to the assembled villagers. The eta melted back, disappearing between two houses as she strode toward the frightened group. She walked slowly, deliberately, head held high. She noticed they shifted uneasily, impressed despite the absurd little dog trotting at her heels.

Rinko halted ten feet from them. There were ten villagers, including Kyoko, who stood in the doorway of her house. Rinko's fingers plucked at the cord that held the yellow silk around the katana. She spoke in her most commanding voice, so their eyes sought her face.

"I will not abandon my father to be devoured by a monster." She noticed several of the villagers wince. "My people don't sacrifice their family out of cowardice. Tonight I'll keep vigil with my father, as is our tradition. In the morning I'll build a pyre and bury his ashes."

"No!" a familiar voice cried. Taro pushed past his mother, his face distraught.

Rinko jerked her gaze from him as another villager, one of the nameless men, spoke. "You don't understand, girl. You'll die!"

"What is this creature, this corpse-eater?" she spat, and the man wilted under her contempt. "Have any of you seen it? No, because you all run and hide when someone dies! You-"

Kyoko caught Taro by the collar and shoved him back into the house. The crowd turned to her expectantly. "You arrogant little fool! You dare to judge us, when you've barely been here a summer? We do what we must to survive! We-"

"Feed your dead to a monster to placate it?"

Kyoko's face flushed red.

"Your elderly cling to life so their bodies won't be desecrated. You don't even build them altars when they die, so you won't be reminded of your shame. And you grew nervous, thinking this creature might move on to the living. So when you saw my father you put us in the house of the dead. And you waited."

Rinko had thought the other villagers would be shocked when she revealed Kyoko's plan. But no one in the little group looked surprised. Even Taro, who'd stuck his head out of the door, only turned his face away.

Rage boiled inside her. No wonder none of these cravens could look her in the eye. Swallowing her anger, she snarled, "I will treat my father with respect." She turned away

Several voices protested at once. One, a woman's, cried, "But you're just a girl!"

She didn't consciously draw her sword, but when she turned back to them the katana was in her hand, the gently curved blade gleaming. The strips of eel leather tied criss-cross over the hilt pressed into her palms. Kana backed away a step, staring at the weapon. Rinko brandished it before her, wrist twisted so they could all see the sunlight glittering on the rippled blade. She saw their expressions shift instantly, from concern to anger to shock.

"I'm not just a girl." She wanted to scream it, to hiss and spit at them like a cat. But she forced her tone to be cold and flat. "I'm samurai."

They stared at her, mouths agape like landed fish. Here at least the samurai still commanded respect. She wanted to slice every one of their stupid heads off, and she could have done it. Each katana's blade was tested on a dead criminal. And these people had no training, no instincts. They would break and run, falling over their own feet, easy pickings. Her fingers tightened on the hilt.

Something touched her shoulder--a human hand, gentle. Before she could turn a voice whispered in her ear. *They're not worth it, daughter.*

Father. The hand vanished as suddenly as it had appeared. A lump rose in Rinko's throat. The villagers were still staring. She swallowed.

"I won't dirty my blade with any of *your* blood," she said harshly. "I will tend to my father."

She left then, sheathing the katana as she did. The walk back to her borrowed house was tense, but Rinio heard nothing but her own and Kana's footsteps. She reached the house and went inside without looking back. Kana lay down in front of the door, head on her paws. The smell of decay was stronger now. She bowed to Father, who had somehow shrunk even further, until he looked like a strange, still child in adult clothes.

There were still a few hours before sunset. Rinko left Kana to guard Father and went into her room. She opened the shutters for some clean air, set the swords gently at the foot of her mat, and tried to sleep.

*

"Rin!"

For one confused moment she thought her father was calling her. Half-asleep, Rinko sat up, rubbing her eyes. Kana curled up by her side, her tail tight against her body. Then Rinko remembered. She recognized this voice, and she wanted nothing to do with him. He hadn't even dared come to the door--his words floated in through the opened window. She kicked off her blanket and rose. As she reached for the shutter, he spoke again. "I should have known you were samurai. You're so..."

"Arrogant?" The bitter word fell from her lips before she could stop it.

The window was above her head, and narrow, so Rinko couldn't see him. But she imagined him, leaning against the outside wall, nervously running his fingers through his hair, searching for a less insulting word.

"...strong," he said. "Rin-"

"My name is Gozen Rinko."

He sighed. "It's not easy, living here in the forest. We do what we have to in order to survive, and we live with the shame of it, Rin...Rinko."

She reached for the shutter. Taro burst out, "We're not like you! No one ever taught us to fight! No one ever taught us to be brave!"

Rinko paused, taken aback by the anguish in his voice. Her hand reached above her head, fingers touching the shutter. She'd never heard Taro sound angry. He'd been kind, only kind...and how much of his mother's plot had he really...?

No. She shook her head to clear it.

"You're right," she said coldly. "We're nothing alike. That's why I will keep vigil with my father while you hide in the forest with the rest of the village."

"You have to come with us, Rinko. You can't stay. Please." His tone was pleading, but she heard defeat in it as well. Suddenly his hand appeared in the window and covered her fingers. She stared at it, her chest hollow. "I...I love you, Rin...Rinko. I can't bear it if anything happens to you."

She pressed her lips together until they hurt. The hollow feeling evaporated. Whatever brief longing she'd felt was gone. "You don't love me enough to stay."

Taro jerked away as if he'd been burned. Even through the wall Rinko could feel his misery. But he said nothing more, and after a moment she heard his sandals moving slowly down the path. Rinko closed and latched the shutters. Kana stood up and stretched. A thin rope of drool dangled from her jaws.

"All right, you're hungry." Rinko went into the main room. She bowed to Father and turned to rummage in the cabinet. Dried fish for Kana, which the dog ate in hurried, grunting gulps. Rinko set up a makeshift altar for Father, folding his other kimono into a precise square and laying it against the wall. She found some dried plums and a handful of rice, which she set on the kimono for offerings. She regretted she had no incense. Kana's nose twitched, but she seemed to understand that the food was forbidden and made no move toward it.

She fetched the swords, secured them to her side, and went outside, Kana at her heels.

No one was visible among the houses. Had they already fled? Night was still an hour away at least. Perhaps they'd run from her wrath. The thought made her smile bitterly.

Rinko couldn't stand still. She circled the house, Kana skittering back and forth to the forest, nose to the ground. Rinko stared into the darkness between the trees, straining until her head ached, but there was nothing, no hint of movement. Only the birds calling mindlessly to each other.

In the garden she weaved between rows of carrots and beans, absently plucking insects from the leaves. There she found tracks. They were larger than her hand, with three stubby toes tipped with a claw as long as her thumb. Rinko thought grimly of the ragged grooves torn into the floor. These were sunk deep into the mud. A creature the size of a bear, Father had said. And she had thought it was at least as large as a tiger. Kana backed away from the prints, refusing to sniff or even go near them.

The sun had sunk below the rooftops, the sky stained pink. They returned to the house. Rinko paused with her hand on the door, looking at Kana.

"You can smell them out," Rinko told her. "You can find their cave and hide with them. You won't do me any good anyway."

Kana trotted past her into the house. Rinko sighed in relief. It was good to not be completely alone, even if her companion was a cowardly little dog.

The scent of decay was even stronger now. Rinko took several deep breaths to overwhelm her sense of smell. She lit a lamp--another gift from Taro, damn him--and unsheathed the swords. She knelt by the wall, across from the door, with the blades lying across her knees. Kana sat beside her, head up, ears alert.

Rinko had left the door open. There was no reason to hide any longer. She gazed past her father, to the rectangle of darkness beyond. A curious calm seized her.

The evening wore on. Kana's head drooped down to her paws. Rinko did not look away from the door. After a while she began composing her death poem in her head. Women didn't need death poems. But warriors did. And now all the other warriors were gone, their world dismantled by the Emperor. She had no way to write it down, but it passed the time.

Hours dragged by in the moonlight that shifted beyond the open door. One, two, three...weariness tugged at her eyelids. Perhaps the creature, realizing she was samurai, had chosen to stay away from this one body? But she couldn't believe it.

She smelled the thing well before she saw it. At first the already-present stink of decomposition masked it, just enough that she thought she might be imagining it. But the smell grew stronger, a stomach-turning stink of rotting fish, stagnant summer ponds, the excrement of a sick animal. She caught her breath, then stopped and forced herself to breathe deeply. Her eyes watered and she blinked the tears away. The swords felt light across her knees. She wrapped her fingers loosely around their hilts. Father lay still, oblivious to the approaching monster. He was lucky he couldn't smell it, Rinko thought wryly. A nervous laugh rose in her throat.

But she didn't laugh, because the corpse-eater appeared in the doorway.

She'd been right about its size. It was as large as a bear, stocky and broad. There was no hair on the scabby hide that stretched over prominent ribs. It had no tail, and each paw was tipped with three curved, catlike claws. A head sat on the hunched shoulders, and it was that which made Rinko's mouth go dry. The face was that of the wizened monk, swollen to an impossible size and elongated into a stubby muzzle. Despite the flattened nose and jaw bristling with jagged yellow teeth, Rinko recognized him. The deep wrinkles and old, sharply slanted eyes were the same.

The monster swung its head from side to side, weirdly human nostrils flaring. Despite the summer heat, Rinko felt a blanket of cold settle over her. She welcomed it, knowing it for the icy, calculating calm the warriors always talked about. The stench, the fear, the anger...all gone. Nothing remained but the samurai and her enemy.

The corpse-eater's gaze found her. At the same moment Rinko rose, the blades of her swords whispering against the skirt of her kimono. The leather that wrapped the hilts pressed into her palms, soaking up sweat. She thought, *Grip them tightly, but not too tightly. Adjust your balance to the weapons' disparate weight.* The thing was thin, but there was power in those legs, in the broad shoulders. Strike for the chest, the belly, the eyes. Avoid the claws. The teeth were a concern, but it had no neck to speak of; the thing's head would not twist easily.

Rinko heard a click behind her--Kana's claws on the floor. For once the little cur wasn't making a racket. Rinko couldn't worry about the dog now--Kana would have to take care of herself. She kept her gaze locked on the corpse-eater as it turned toward her.

Lips drew back from cracked teeth. The monk's eyes glittered in the low firelight. Rinko's heart tried to speed up, but she forced it to slow, back into its old steady rhythm.

"You." The creature's voice was a mixture of the monk's high pitch and an animal's growl. Kana whined urgently.

"Yes." Rinko's voice cut off the dog's whimpering. "Me."

It surveyed the room. When it saw her father, a long, thin rope of drool dropped from its jaws, swinging in the firelight. Rinko bit back her disgust. Every muscle in her body felt tight, coiled like a snake.

"Go." The creature jerked its hungry gaze from Father's corpse with obvious effort.

Rinko didn't waste breath on a reply. Slowly she shook her head. The monster cast another hungry look at the corpse. Rinko took advantage of its averted gaze and charged it. It must have seen her movement from the corner of its vision, for it dodged her jab and rounded on her, hissing like a cat. Rinko backed away, swords at the ready. She hadn't expected to strike it; she'd been testing its range of movement.

"Move aside." The thing's jaws barely moved when it spoke.

Rinko silently shook her head.

"He's dead flesh." The creature's tone took on a wheedling quality that grated against her taut nerves. "He feels nothing. Save yourself."

"He's my father."

They regarded each other in the flickering light. The creature heaved a shuddering sigh that flooded the room with the stink of rotten meat. It lowered its head and lunged at her.

Rinko held her ground. At the last moment, as she dug her bare toes into the floor and braced for impact, the creature swerved. One paw struck the floor dangerously near to Father's head. Rinko swiped at it with the katana, and the thing yanked its leg back with a moan. A few drops of black blood spattered the floor.

Rinko's eyes narrowed. It could feel pain. A grim smile curved her lips.

The creature lurched toward Father, and again Rinko drove it off. They stalked around Father's still form, the firelight throwing their shadows crazily against the wall. Rinko's mind raced. Her eyes saw everything unnaturally clear. She focused solely on the corpse-eater, allowing all else to be swallowed up in shadow. She just had to wait for it to tire, to do something stupid. It was desperate, anyone could see that, and desperation made humans stupid. And it was still human, somewhere inside.

It lunged several times as if to sink its teeth into the withered flesh, and each time Rinko repelled it. Surely it knew it couldn't get past her swords. Like her, it was looking for a weakness. She was determined to disappoint it.

The thing darted at her, faster than Rinko had expected. One paw came up to strike at her. Her muscles reacted without thought. She threw herself forward, at the same time dropping to her knees so she skidded beneath the deadly claws. Her kimono split open below the obi, and a burning sensation told her both her knees were skinned. But it felt distant, as if the pain and trickling blood belonged to someone else. Instantly she was on her feet again, twisting to face the creature's unprotected flank. She thrust the katana forward, aiming between the prominent ribs. But it suddenly kicked out with its back legs like an angry horse. One set of claws caught in her kimono skirt. The fabric tore and dragged the ground, exposing her wounded knees. The blow deflected her thrust just enough that her blade left only a deep scratch in the scabbed skin.

Kana exploded out of the corner where she'd been cowering, barking with hysterical ferocity. Rinko, used to the dog's sudden fits, barely noticed her until the monster started and backed away, distracted by her yapping. It snapped at Kana, swinging its muzzle into her side. The dog fell over but immediately bounced up again. Rinko raised her swords, but the corpse-eater lunged toward Kana, claw-tipped toes curved like fingers around the little dog's neck. Kana's growling rose to a yelp, then a shriek, then faded to gurgling as the thing pinned her to the floor. The dog's rear legs thrashed. *It hasn't killed her yet,* Rinko thought coldly. It would have been simpler for it to get rid of the little annoyance. Rinko wished for a naginata, the long, broad-bladed spear all samurai women learned to wield. With it she could have struck it before it snapped Kana's neck. She pushed the thought aside. Concentrate on what *is*. Kana would die, but so would the corpse-eater. Rinko planted her feet and readied herself to charge.

Yet she didn't. Why? She surveyed the situation. Kana's eyes rolled in panic, showing their whites. The corpse-eater held her steady. It raised its head to look at her, and Rinko knew why she'd hesitated.

Rinko chanced a glance away from the thing's head and saw its front leg jerking convulsively, as if something held it down. The creature stood in the spot where she'd noticed the claw marks, months ago. By chance it had sunk its foot in the same place, and it had put all its weight on that foot when it caught Kana. Now those wicked claws were trapped deep in the splintered floorboards. She almost laughed, but didn't. She couldn't dismiss any enemy until its head was impaled on a pike before the gate.

The creature must have seen her gaze flicker past it. Its blackened lips drew back. "You're samurai. Educated. You know what irony is?"

"I know what honor is. You have none. Nor do any of these peasants. You're well-suited for each other."

"You're right." The corpse-eater lowered its head, but its eyes remained on Rinko and her swords. A low moan escaped its throat. Kana whimpered. "It's an ugly tale, but a short one. Will you hear it, Lady Samurai? And then put an end to my suffering? It's been so long."

Rinko regarded it warily. She didn't want to listen to anything this monster had to say. But it had addressed her by her proper title. It had bowed, as well as it could, and shown respect. "Release the dog."

"I will, Lady Samurai. I know you will keep your word." It lifted its foot, and Kana skittered away, gasping. Rinko didn't watch her go. "I was a monk, once. But I didn't serve the gods. Oh, I started out that way. Some are forced into the temples by their families or their circumstances. Not me. I was drawn to a life of quiet, and work, and prayer. I was so devoted that when the old abbot died the others clamored for me to be put in his place. I found myself directing a monastery, and that was when everything began to go wrong."

Rinko hadn't lowered her weapons. An ache bloomed in her shoulders; she ignored it. All her nerves hummed with tension. Silently she waited for the thing to stop talking so she could kill it.

"As an abbot, I learned about wealth and power. People came to with problems, with questions--and with hands full of offerings. I quickly found that I could give orders, make demands...and that ignorant people will do anything to ensure a blessing from the gods.

"For years I lived like that, pretending to be a holy man while hoarding wealth, taking women. My monks knew. But the ones who cared, what could they do? Only death could remove me from my post. Death or the gods. And finally they decided I'd sinned enough."

A trickle of sweat started in Rinko's hair and raced down her neck. But the creature still wasn't finished.

"One of my monks died. I went to pray over him and was seized by...hunger. I fought it, but...they found me crouched over him, changed into what you see. They would have killed me, despite their vows, so I fled before they could. I struggled into the forest. As the sun rose, I changed back into my human form. I realized I was cursed, and I didn't have to wonder why.

"I wandered, eating when I found something dead, that monstrous hunger always gnawing at me. You can't imagine the torment..."

Rinko flicked her wrist, just a fraction. The katana caught the dying light, and the creature's eyes widened. "I came to this place after a long time. By luck one of the villagers had just died, some fool who fell and cracked open his head. The body lay alone in this house, the night before his cremation. You know what followed."

She nodded. As it talked, she'd been seeking the best spot to slash. She couldn't see the thing's throat. Through the eye would be quick and simple. Rinko had never killed anything before, despite all her training. "Are you finished?"

"Yes." A grin slowly cracked the horrible face. The corpse-eater rose up on its hind legs, and Rinko saw that it had been stalling. While it talked it had been working its toes, weakening the wood that trapped it. Now it tore free, yanking the floor board loose with a ripping sound. The board splintered and snapped. The creature rose, the section of floor still impaled on its claws.

She hadn't guessed that it could stand on two legs. *Stupid!* Reared up like that, it was a full six inches taller than a man, far taller than Rinko. The massive paws were raised to the height of her head. The corpse-eater gave a strange, convulsive jerk of its leg. The board flew from its claws and shot toward Rinko. She jerked out of the way, but not quickly enough. A corner of the wood struck her temple, yanking her head back. She kept her balance, but only just. There was pain and something hot trickling over her face, but it was distant. The board struck the wall behind her with a dull thud and clattered to the floor. The thing threw itself at her with a hoarse scream. Rinko brought both swords up but it was already in front of her, moving with a speed she hadn't anticipated. Rinko swung her blades. The shorter wakizashi missed. The katana did not.

    The blade was so sharp that she felt hardly any resistance as it sheared through the thing's toes. The claws fell to the floor in a triple spurt of blood. The sharp metallic stench of blood filled the room. The corpse-eater howled, an eerie cry somewhere between human and animal. It swung at her with its mutilated paw, spraying Rinko with warm blood. The taste of salt and metal flooded her mouth. She dodged, trying to spit the thing's blood out as she ducked. There was movement in the corner of her vision, and Kana flew past, a silent blur of black and gray. She sank her teeth into one of its rear legs. It snarled and swatted her with its good front paw. Kana held fast, but a second blow broke her grip and sent her skidding across the floor on her side. She struck the wall and lay still.

    Rinko turned to look at her dog, her icy focus cracked. The corpse-eater struck her arm with its heavy head. Her fingers, cramped from holding the katana so long, jerked involuntarily open. The sword fell to the floor. Rinko gasped as if she'd been punched. The creature struck her with its bleeding paw, catching her shoulder. Rinko spun but kept her feet...until the thing crashed into her and bore her face-first to the floor.

    Pain exploded in her cheekbone as she struck. The creature was heavier than its gaunt frame implied. It crushed her, suffocating. Every breath brought a stab of agony in her side. Everything else was numb. The thing's chill breath stirred the hair on the back of her neck. With her face pressed into the floorboards, Rinko could see only vague movement as the thing's elongated jaw opened. Cold slaver dripped onto her skin. It had her pinned. Helpless.

    No, not completely pinned, she realized as feeling slowly crept back into her body. One arm was free from the elbow--the creature's toeless paw couldn't grasp her wrist as the other one did. Her free hand still clutched the wakizashi.

Rinko sucked in a pain-riddled breath. Something cracked in her shoulder as she twisted her arm unnaturally backwards. The tip of the wakizashi struck something solid that parted beneath its tip. The corpse-eater jerked. It gave a strangled cry. She yanked her wrist painfully in order to twist the blade and drive it deeper. Its body heaved and pulsed as it struggled for air. The creature exhaled a long, whining breath that ended in a rattle. It collapsed on her, driving all the air from her lungs. Its head lay on the floor by her shoulder; Rinko was briefly glad her head was trapped facing the other direction, so she didn't have to look at it. Her free arm dropped to the floor. She could no longer tell if her numb fingers held the wakizashi.

The stench was overpowering. Rinko gagged as she tried to wiggle her other arm. Nothing. She could barely move her fingers. One of her legs was uncovered to the knee, but it was useless. Her chest ached and her breathing was shallow and painful. Her face felt hot and swollen, and her mouth tasted of blood. Would she have to languish here until those craven peasants finally crept back? Or would she suffocate first? She could see the door, tauntingly far away.

A small face appeared in Rinko's vision, watching her with bright eyes. A pink tongue lolled out and reached Rinko's face. Kana limped on one leg, but she seemed otherwise unhurt. Rinko smiled in relief, though she was too crushed to say the dog's name. Kana sat by her head. Rinko breathed in her warm, dusty smell.

The door crashed open. Kana jumped up, barking. Rinko painfully craned her neck to see Taro in the doorway, outlined by the dim firelight. He brandished a wooden hoe in one hand.

"Rinko!" He looked around frantically. For a moment he froze, gaping at the dead creature. Then he saw Rinko and ran to her, gagging as the thing's smell struck him. When he'd finished retching he gasped, "You...you killed it?"

"Get it off me." It hurt to say even that much.

It took some time. Taro built up the fire first, wincing as the flames showed him more of the creature. Kana danced around, yapping uselessly, as he shoved and maneuvered and finally used the hoe as a lever to heave the thing over. It slumped on its back with a final, sick thump. The leather wrappings on the hilts were soaked dark red. Taro leaned over her. "Are you hurt?"

What a stupid question. Every inch of her body hurt, each individual ache bleeding together into a solid mass of pain. Breathing was easier now, but each gasp brought a stab of agony in her side. Perhaps she'd broken a rib, or several. For a few moments Rinko couldn't move, no matter how much she willed it. Just as panic hooked its claws into her mind, one knee bent. Then the other, with an audible crack. Fingers next, elbows. Finally she raised her head a little. Taro hovered over her like a nursemaid. Rinko closed her eyes and concentrated on easing herself up bit by bit, pausing when the knife in her side twisted. Kana paced around the thing, sniffing furiously, brave now it was dead. The wakizashi's blade had penetrated the fold between the creature's shoulder and head. A pool of dark red blood cooled on the floor where it had lain.

Slowly she got to her feet, halting and creaking like a very old woman. Once standing she took Taro's proffered arm, gripping tightly until a wave of dizziness passed. Now that his fears were alleviated, his resolve seemed to falter. He stared at the corpse-eater, his face gray and drawn, his arm trembling beneath her fingers.

Rinko looked down at herself. Her braid was unraveled, her hair matted with blood. Her kimono was sticky with it.

"What do we do now?" Taro sounded lost.

"Swords," Rinko rasped. She pulled away from him.

"I'll get them!" Taro turned to the carcass.

"Don't touch them!" She limped to the katana. Bending to retrieve the weapon was agony, but Rinko held her breath and didn't exhale until both wakizashi and katana were in her hands.

"My mother begged me not to come," Taro said. "I told her I'm a man now, and I refused to hide anymore."

Rinko would have laughed if her side wasn't so painful. "You found your courage too late."

"No one else came!" He sounded like a hurt child.

"When will the rest of them come back?" She turned toward the door. Taro hurried to take the lantern and follow. The night air was warm and clean and didn't smell of corruption. Rinko wished her ribs would allow her to take deep breaths.

"They're waiting for me to come back and tell them it's safe. If I don't, I suppose they'll come after the sun rises. That's the usual way."

"How long until sunrise?" It hurt too much to tilt back her head and see the position of the moon.

"Three hours, at least."

"Then I'm going to your bath house."

It took a long time to make her way there, and longer to clean some of the stinking blood from her skin and clothes. When she finally felt tolerably clean and a bit rested, Rinko started back to the house.

After the reprieve, the stench inside the house was worse than ever. Taro lingered by the door. "Why do you want to go back in there?"

Rinko didn't bother answering. She limped inside and went to Father. Kneeling was too difficult, so she had to be content with merely glancing over his body. Despite the battle and the rotting carcass that lay so near, his body was untouched, without so much as a splash of blood on his robe. She managed the slightest of bows.

"Please make sure my father is properly buried, or cremated. Your village owes him that. If you...love me, like you claim, you'll do this for my father. Your village has to build its own cemetery again, or find your old one if you can."

He glanced toward the house. "Rin...I mean, Rinko, what do we do about the...monster?"

"I don't care. It's your village's creature, they can decide what to do with it. My work is finished."

"They'll be so grateful, Rinko. You're a hero! They'll do anything you-"

"I don't want anything from them!" Rinko snarled. Taro snapped his mouth shut, flinching away as if she'd threatened to hit him. "I don't want anything from a bunch of cringing cowards!"

Taro's lips twitched. In a cajoling tone he said, "But you like Kana..."

"Kana stayed."

Kana sat beside Taro, watching as Rinko limped around the fallen monster and its congealing blood. It was already decaying, the skin clinging tighter to the bones, drying and darkening. The glassy eyes had sunk deep in their sockets. She gathered up blankets, sandals, coins--everything she and Father had brought with them. She moved slowly, gasping in shallow breaths. In the bath house she'd tied a cloth tightly around her ribs, which helped a bit, but her side still hurt badly. She took all the food in the house. She found Father's worn peasant hat and pulled it down over her head. She looked at Kana. "Are you coming?"

For answer the little dog hopped out the door and stood in the path, tail wagging. Rinko turned her back on the borrowed house and the rotting thing within. By afternoon this cursed place would be far behind her. She regretted leaving Father here, but there was no other choice.

Of course Taro followed her outside, twisting his hands anxiously. "Rin? What-"

"Thank you for your help this summer. We're leaving now."

"You're leaving? Now? But Rinko...you're hurt. And all alone, at night. You can stay here, you can...live here. I mean...where else can you go?"

"Anywhere but here." She took the lantern from his unresisting fingers.

"Wait! Rinko!" He hesitated a moment. When she and Kana reached the tree line, Rinko glanced back in time to see him ducking into his mother's house.

She held up the lantern as far as her injured ribs allowed, letting it swing until she found a break in the trees. They'd go just far enough to shed this village's dirt from their feet, then rest until morning.

"Follow me," she told Kana, and entered the forest.

*

Twenty days after Father's death, Rinko and Kana came to a town called Oshima. It had a bustling market. Rinko wandered down the aisles, looking for any necessities she could spend her few remaining coins on. She'd learned that farmers were usually willing to hire help for a day or two, but most could only pay in food and shelter for a night.

The swords were strapped across her back, and she reached up--her ribs ached only dully now--to touch the silken cloth wrapped around the katana's hilt. No one out here seemed to notice the strangely-shaped bundles. For them the samurai were a distant dream, and a dream they would remain. It saddened her, but Rinko found her resentment was fading. She had no time for it now. Winter was coming, and she had to decide where to go and if she would stay there.

She glanced over her shoulder. There he was, half-hidden behind a burly man carrying a sake barrel. Rinko had noticed him following them two days after they'd left the village. She was certain he'd seen Father buried, as she'd asked. He wouldn't have dared to track her if he hadn't... no, that wasn't fair. Taro would have made sure Father was buried because he *did* have a sense of honor, even if it wasn't as highly developed as a samurai's.

She'd only seen him in glimpses since leaving the village; a quick movement as he peered out from behind a boulder, or a flash of his kimono as he tried to melt into a crowded street. At night, as she and Kana huddled close to their fire, she could feel him camping just over the last rise or down a hill, in a copse of trees. Taro had proven himself to be a good tracker. She could have called to him at any time, invited him to share their fire and food. But she hadn't. Winter was coming, but she still had enough time to make her choices.

The smell of boiling noodles caught her attention from the next aisle over. Kana's tongue hung out, dripping. Clutching her coin, Rinko strode forward, looking forward to having something hot to eat.

End

Patricia Correll lives in Kentucky with her family and cats. She is the author of numerous short stories as well as the novella collection Late Summer, Early Spring (DSP Publications, 2015). You can find her on the web at https://www.facebook.com/authorpatriciacorrell/ and on Twitter at @Author_PCorrell

Made in the USA
Columbia, SC
14 May 2024